MAY 5

DEMCO

Disney's

American Frontier #10

WILD BILL HICKOK
AND THE REBEL RAIDERS

A Historical Novel

by Ron Fontes and Justine Korman
Illustrations by Charlie Shaw
Cover illustration by Dave Henderson

DISNEP PRESS

NEW YORK

Look for these other books in the
American Frontier series:

Davy Crockett and the King of the River

Davy Crockett and the Creek Indians

Davy Crockett and the Pirates at Cave-in Rock

Davy Crockett at the Alamo

Johnny Appleseed and the Planting of the West

Davy Crockett and the Highwaymen

Sacajawea and the Journey to the Pacific

Calamity Jane at Fort Sanders

Annie Oakley in the Wild West Extravaganza!

Tecumseh: One Nation for His People

Davy Crockett Meets Death Hug

FIRST EDITION
1   3   5   7   9   10   8   6   4   2

Library of Congress Catalog Card Number: 92-56159
ISBN: 1-56282-493-7 / 1-56282-494-5 (lib. bdg.)

Consultant: Joseph W. Snell, Executive Director Emeritus
Kansas State Historical Society
Topeka, Kansas

CHAPTER 1

He's late," Hickok said, tucking a gold watch into the pocket of his buckskins. From the porch of the Rock Creek station house Hickok gazed out over the low Nebraska hills, waiting impatiently for signs of a rider. But there was no column of dust, no familiar *whoop*, nothing that might signal the approach of a pony express rider. Hickok's hands strayed idly to the guns that poked out from a red silk sash around his waist. He wore the gun butts forward. "For the quick draw," it was said.

Bob Mills, a young relief rider, nervously patted the neck of his restless pony. "Do you think there's trouble, Mr. Hickok?" he asked.

Hickok nodded. "Trouble."

Inside the station house, Clancy, another young rider, began to play a harmonica. When he saw Hickok in the doorway he stopped.

"I've been workin' on 'O Susanna,' Mr. Hickok," Clancy said. "Care to get out your fiddle?" Clancy watched Hickok fill a flask with powder, then a pouch with lead balls. He also tucked a box of firing caps into a satchel. Obviously, Hickok was in no mood for fiddle music. Clancy stuffed the harmonica in his pocket and followed Hickok outside.

Hickok crossed to the corral, swung open the gate, and walked into the barn. Inside, thirteen-year-old Luke Harte sat on a bale of hay reading a book. At the sound of Hickok's approach Luke dropped the book and jumped to his feet. "Sorry, Mr. Hickok," he said guiltily. "But I finished my chores, and besides, this part is so exciting! Y'see, Deadeye Dick's been trapped by hostiles who've—"

Hickok held up a hand. "Saddle Nell," he told the boy.

In Luke's eyes James Hickok was larger than life. Larger even than the heroes in his dime novels. Bigger than Deadeye Dick. Hickok was more than six feet tall, with long, wavy chestnut-colored hair that fell to his shoulders. A full mustache drooped over his thin lips.

"Yes, sir!" Luke said, running to fetch Hickok's saddle. A rack of saddles hung on a wall. Each saddle had been oiled and polished. Luke knew that the pony express rider had only one job: carry the mail from one frontier outpost to the next. And ride as fast as the wind in between. It was his job to make sure the horses were ready to go at a moment's notice, day or night, rain or shine.

Luke led Nell from the corral. Hickok was standing outside the barn door. Luke cinched the saddle girth, then patted Nell's flank.

"Are you going after the rider?" Luke asked Hickok excitedly as he handed him the reins. "I can come, too. It won't take a minute to get ready. Then if there's trouble, I could ride for help."

A slight grin flitted across the corners of Hickok's mouth, but he shook his head.

"Do you think he was jumped by desperadoes? Or maybe a bobcat?" Luke asked. "He might've been bit by a snake, too. Or lamed his horse in a prairie dog hole, or—"

Luke broke off as Hickok swung up into Nell's saddle.

Hickok checked the loads in his pistols. "Are you thinking he was attacked by the Chambers gang?" Luke asked.

Hickok nodded. "Maybe," he said.

"Chambers and his gang of rebel raiders are just about the worst bunch of thieves in the territory," Clancy said. "Got the farmers around here near about scared to death."

Luke gave a low whistle. "Grandpa said they hanged a man just for the heck of it!"

Hickok pursed his lips. "A right inconsiderate bunch, I'd say," Hickok drawled matter-of-factly.

Luke peered down at his scuffed boots. "With all due respect," Luke said earnestly, "you oughtn't to ride out alone." He moved to fetch a saddle from the wall.

"I can come, too," Clancy said.

Hickok waved Clancy off. "Ain't no need. Thanks all the same."

He turned to look down at Luke. "Stay with the horses," Hickok said. Without another word, he rode off.

From the barn door, Luke watched the black mare gallop away in a cloud of dust. "Sure wish I could've gone with him," he said. After a time he settled back on the hay bale and picked up his dog-eared copy of *The Fabulous Aventures of Deadeye Dick*. He read a few pages, then put the book down. "It just ain't fair," he moped. "How come my life ain't never as exciting as the stories in books?"

CHAPTER 2

"Whoa, Nell," Hickok called, and the mare obediently came to a stop. Hickok squinted, trying to bring into focus the lone figure that appeared in the distance. Whoever it was, the figure was on foot.

Just in case the figure was not a friendly one, Hickok freed one pistol from his sash.

Trust nothing and no one, Hickok had learned. He had learned that the hard way.

Hickok gave Nell the word and they cautiously set forward.

Hickok grinned to himself when he recognized the dusty figure coming toward him. It was a young pony express rider by the name of William F. Cody. Hickok tucked the pistol back into his sash and gave a loud whistle. The rider waved.

"Nice of you to drop by," Cody said calmly as Hickok rode up. A mail pouch and saddle were hoisted over his shoulder.

"Well, well," Hickok said, grinning. He uncorked

his canteen and handed it to Cody. "Trouble?" he asked simply.

"Trouble?" he repeated. "I was only jumped by fifty of the meanest owlhoots this side of Hades!"

"Is that a fact," Hickok said.

Cody nodded. "I fought like a cornered bobcat," he said, swinging his fists left and right. "I must've drawn blood from at least five of 'em before I dented someone's gun butt with the back of my head."

Hickok leaned his arms over the saddle horn. The kid hasn't changed a bit, Hickok thought to himself. Hickok had first met Cody in Kansas in 1859. He was a wonder at spinning tales even then, Hickok remembered. The Cody family owned a boarding house in Leaven-worth County, Kansas, and it was as a boarder there that Hickok had first met young William, then age thirteen.

"When I came to," Cody went on, "my horse was gone, but they'd left the saddle and mail pouch. I guess they figured that keeping those might be evidence."

"Sounds like the work of Jack Chambers, all right," Hickok said, pulling on the edges of his mustache.

Cody looked up at Hickok and squinted. "You tangle with these boys before?" he asked, shielding his eyes with his hand.

Hickok shook his head. "Not yet," he said. "But I heard plenty about him and his brother already. They're supposed to be plenty mean," Hickok said, "but not too bright. Especially the brother, Heck." Hickok smiled and looked thoughtfully off into the distance, as if an interesting thought had just occurred to him. "Of course,"

he said, tugging again at his mustache, "they did manage somehow to separate a smart feller like you from your horse, so I guess they can't be all *that* stupid."

Cody rolled his eyes. "You going to give me a lecture, Mr. Hickok, or a ride back to the station?"

"That's a right fair question, Mr. Cody. The fact is, maybe I should make you walk back to Rock Creek to teach you a lesson."

Cody snorted and shrugged. "Suit yourself, old man."

"*Old* man!" Hickok repeated playfully, shaking his head. Hickok had only recently turned twenty-three.

"Well," Cody said, "it is true enough you're too old to be a pony express rider." He stopped and gave Hickok an appraising glance. "And too fat."

Hickok pretended to be offended. "Anyway," Cody pointed out, "I'm still the best rider in the pony express."

"Uh-huh," Hickok said, grinning. "Hop on then. I can't be having the fastest and best rider in the whole dang express delivering the mail on foot!" He reached down to help Cody up into the saddle. Hickok gave a slight tug to Nell's reins, and she broke into a gallop.

"I'd heard you'd taken over the Rock Creek station," Cody said. He figured conversation might help pass the time. "Also heard you were almost killed by a grizzly bear you fought off with your bare hands."

"Cinnamon bear," Hickok called out over his shoulder. "And I had some help." He drew an enormous bowie knife from his sash. The blade winked in the sun. Hickok carefully tucked it away.

"I *also* heard talk that you were getting a reputation as the fastest shot in the Nebraska territory."

"The way you rattle on," Hickok said with a hint of irritation, "I'm surprised you got time to hear anything at all."

Cody took the hint and reluctantly settled back for a quiet ride to the station. I just hope it ain't a long trip, he thought.

"Rider!" Luke hollered as Hickok came into view.

Bob Mills held the reins of his pony steady. He was ready to ride.

Hickok tossed Bob the leather mail pouch—the *mochila*—and Bob swung it easily over the pony's saddle. Because speed was all important to the pony express, a pouch never weighed more than twenty pounds. The letters, usually written on tissue paper, were wrapped in oiled silk to keep them dry. For a service that delivered letters across the country in just ten days, folks paid the hefty sum of five dollars for each ounce.

"Horse thieves," Hickok warned as Bob spurred his mount. "Keep your eyes open."

Bob waved, then was gone in a cloud of dust.

"What happened?" Luke asked.

"You'd be better off asking what didn't happen," Cody said. "This was almost the most exciting ride I've made!"

Hickok turned to Luke. "Take care of Nell while Mr. Cody washes up for dinner."

"Dinner!" Cody exclaimed. "Why, I could eat a bushel of rattlesnakes—raw!"

"That won't be necessary," Hickok said. "Luke here is a fine cook."

The boy blushed. "Yeah, well, I ain't gonna be a cook and stableboy forever," he declared. "I'm going to be a rider as soon as I'm old enough."

"That won't be long," Cody assured Luke. Cody was only fifteen himself, even though most riders were eighteen.

"Are you good with horses?" Cody asked.

"I'm okay, I guess," he said sheepishly.

"He's very good," Hickok said, "when he isn't reading or jawing."

Luke led Nell back to the barn. "And pump some water for Mr. Cody," Hickok called after him.

Cody followed Luke to the pump. "Ain't at *all* like it is in books," Luke mumbled.

"How's that?" Cody asked.

Luke sighed. "Nuthin'."

Hickok looked up as Cody stomped into the station house.

"Nothin' like cold water to wake a man up," Cody brayed.

With the dust washed off his face, William F. Cody's skin was a few shades lighter.

"That cooking smells almost as good as my mother's," Cody said eagerly. "I can't wait to sink my teeth into it. Back at the Big Sandy station all they've got is salt pork and hardtack. A person can't hardly hold body and soul together with such fare." He dropped into a chair and tucked a checkered napkin under his chin.

Clancy ambled into the station and flopped onto the chair across from Cody. Luke brought steaming platters of food to the table. Cody pounced on his like a cat on a fat field mouse. His knife was never still. When it wasn't loaded with squash, Cody would wave it to emphasize a point. He talked and talked and talked—first about his exploits fighting hostile Indian tribes, then about working on an army supply wagon train, and now about riding for the pony express.

"Mr. Cody," Luke gasped, "ain't you a might young to've done all that?"

Cody grinned. "That ain't the half of it."

"Ever thought of going on the stage?" Hickok asked with amused sarcasm during a rare pause in Cody's monologue. "You put on quite a show."

"Why, this is nothing!" Cody grinned. "Wait till I tell you about the time I—"

Hickok held up his hand. "Slow down. Let's get back to business. Fifty men ambushed you?"

"At least ten," Cody amended.

"Did you leave a mark on any of 'em?"

A faint blush rose to Cody's cheeks. "Maybe nothing the constable could use as proof. I did kick at a couple, but I was too passed out to do much good."

"What did they look like?"

Cody licked the chicken grease off his fingers

thoughtfully. "Didn't see much before they dropped me, mainly just the ground coming up to greet me. But I did notice the leader wore a long, tan duster coat, the kind gentlemen wear to keep their clothes clean when they ride."

"That's got to be Jack Chambers and his rebel raiders!" Luke exclaimed. "Jack has some of the orneriest varmints in the territory riding with him! Cockeyed Frank and Turkey Creek Jack, the Widowmaker, and Shorty Collins. They call Jack the Undertaker's Friend!"

"Figures, or they wouldn't have had a chance against me," Cody bragged. "Well, who is this Chambers feller anyway?" he asked.

"Grandpa says him and his raiders are just a bunch of no-good thieves. He says Chambers is sympathetic to the folks who want to keep slaves, and he steals horses from antislavers. With the war on between the North and the South, Chambers and his bunch are stealing horses from antislavers to sell to rebel armies."

Luke broke off for a moment. He was a little embarrassed. He had never talked so much before, or with such force.

"Grandpa calls slavery an abomination!" Luke blurted.

Cody nearly choked on his food. "An aboma*what*?"

"Abomination," Luke repeated. "I guess it means slavery is against the Bible."

"I don't know about that," Clancy said. "All I know is—slavery or no—folks is gettin' mighty riled up. It's like you can't take a breath anymore without someone jumping down your throat about it. Just the other day I saw a feller nearly get his head broke on account of him being against slavery." Clancy shook his head disgustedly. "Personally, I just don't see what all the fuss is about."

Cody waved a fork at Clancy. "The point is folks got a right to be free."

"Says who?" Clancy asked.

Cody worked his mouth around a forkful of food. "Abe Lincoln, that's who!"

Clancy shrugged. "Yankee presidents don't mean much to folks around here. You tell planters they can't have their slaves, they'd just as soon shoot you as look at you."

"Maybe," Cody said. "Maybe not. But just 'cause some planters have got a need don't make it right."

"Who's right is the man carrying the gun," Clancy shot back.

Hickok winced. Ever since he had left Illinois a few years back and had crossed through Kansas and Nebraska looking for farmland to settle, it had been the same argument. Some folks wanted to keep slaves; some folks didn't. Opinions had grown as hard as Nebraska flatland in January.

The worst part, Hickok thought, was that the law in the territory was unreliable at best. It was still a wild and untamed wilderness where most often men would settle arguments not in a courtroom but through the barrel of a gun. A town might not have a circuit-court judge visit but once a year—or less often. Folks would get impatient and take the law into their own hands.

"Might makes right, is that it?" Cody asked Clancy.

"I ain't saying it's right," Clancy said defensively. "All I'm saying is a man with a gun makes a better argument than a man without. Shoot, look at Chambers and his bunch. They practically run Fairbury."

Luke jumped in. "My grandpa says folks in town should stand up to Chambers. He says Chambers ain't no better than a common criminal."

Clancy scoffed. "Stand up to Jack Chambers! Shoot, those folks are afeard of their own shadow. How else can you explain Jack and his boys livin' like a bunch of bankers out there on that ranch of his? Why, if they had any gumption at all, they'd run his yellow hide right out of town!"

"That's mighty big talk," Cody said. "You ever go up against this Jack Chambers feller yourself?"

"Well, not exactly," Clancy had to admit.

"I didn't think so," Cody said with a smirk.

"You calling me a coward?" Clancy snarled.

"What I'm saying is, talk is cheap," Cody shot back.

Hickok pushed himself up from the table. "I've heard enough," he said angrily. He looked hard at each one of them. "Right now I ain't interested in causes or debates or who's right or who's wrong. What I'm interested in *now* is the whereabouts of Mr. Cody's horse."

CHAPTER 3

Hickok rode Nell to the town of Fairbury, about five miles from Rock Creek station. Fairbury was not much more than a rutted dirt road flanked by two rows of one- and two-story buildings. The constable's office was a small brick building next to the bank.

A bell jangled as Hickok stepped inside the office. Constable Jody Lee sat up abruptly and rubbed the palms of his hands against his eyes.

"Well, well," he said, leaning back in his chair. "If it ain't Mr. Hickok himself." His eyes were small and black like a snake's. "To what do I owe this honor?" A half-empty bottle sat open on the edge of his desk.

For some reason Hickok couldn't understand, Lee had developed an instant dislike for Hickok.

Maybe it was that Hickok had earned a reputation as an honest constable in Kansas. Whatever the reason, Hickok was only too willing to return the favor.

He disliked Lee and thought him lazy and dishonest. "I come on business," Hickok said.

Lee stroked his mustache thoughtfully. "Is that a

fact? And what business might that be? One of your riders stub a toe?" Lee burst out laughing.

Lee flipped forward in his chair and poured himself a drink. He swallowed the drink quickly and wiped a greasy shirtsleeve across his lips.

"Looks like Chambers has stolen one of my riders' horses," Hickok said.

Lee looked doubtful. "That don't sound like Jack Chambers to me. What kind of proof you got?"

"One of my riders said—"

"Can't arrest a man on hearsay, Hickok." Lee settled back in his chair and scratched his head. "You got anything else? Something that might stand up in court?"

"All the proof we need is in Chambers's corral. Pony express horses carry the company brand."

Lee turned his hands up in a gesture of helplessness.

"Well now, Mr. Hickok, you being a former lawman and all, you should know I can't go riding out to Chambers's place on just someone's say so. Who's to say your boy didn't lose his horse and blame it on poor Jack Chambers?"

"The horse is in his corral. Take my word for it."

"*Your* word?" Lee said. "Jack Chambers has lived around these parts for years. Why should I take your word over his?"

"Chambers is a thief and you know it," Hickok said hotly.

"What I know," Lee shot back, "is that Jack Chambers sells horses. Ain't nothing illegal about that."

"It is if those horses are stolen."

"These are confusing and lawless times, Mr. Hickok," Lee explained in the condescending tone a teacher might use with a child. "The whole dang country has torn itself apart. North versus South. Slavers versus abolitionists. People shooting one another down in the street."

"I ain't interested in a history lesson," Hickok drawled. "I'm only interested in my horse."

Lee shrugged. "It ain't that simple," he said.

Hickok couldn't believe what he was hearing. "You mean to tell me you ain't going to do nothing about this?"

"I done tried to tell you," Lee said. "Ain't nothing to *be* done. It ain't my fault your boy ain't got enough sense to keep himself strapped into the saddle."

"That horse didn't wander off," Hickok said. "It was stolen."

"That's what *you* say." Lee sat back with another jigger from the bottle on his desk and tapped a finger on the tin star on his shirt. "What *I* say is the horse wandered off. And I'm the law around here."

Hickok glowered at Lee. "You ain't any more the law in this town than I am the king of France."

Lee drank, shrugged, and folded his hands across his belly. "Suit yourself, Hickok. But I'll give you one bit of friendly advice. Don't go messin' with Jack Chambers. It ain't neighborly, if you get my meaning."

Hickok understood perfectly. Lee was one of Chambers's hired guns. It wasn't uncommon in some parts of the territory to buy a lawman's services. If you pay some men enough money, they'll look the other way.

Hickok figured a constable as lazy as Lee probably didn't cost Chambers much. Anything he wanted done, Lee would do. Hickok had seen lawmen like Lee before. If anything was to be done about Jack Chambers, he would have to do it himself.

"Thanks for nothing," Hickok said as he turned toward the door.

Lee gave Hickok an oily smile. "Anytime."

Jack Chambers was enjoying the late afternoon sunshine when Hickok rode up. At Hickok's approach he rose from a rocking chair and stood on the front steps of his farmhouse with his feet apart and his arms crossed over his barrel chest. A pair of well-polished revolvers gleamed at his waist. Behind him on the porch two men sat playing cards on a low table.

"Help you, stranger?" he asked.

Chambers's eyes immediately went to the red silk sash and the ivory-handled guns. He pushed back the brim of his hat and whistled.

"Mighty fancy duds you got on, mister. Is this a business call, or has the circus come to town?"

He grinned and looked over his shoulder to his brother, Hector, who had walked up from the corral and now stood behind him. Heck cut himself a large chunk of tobacco and crammed it into his mouth.

"Say, Heck," Jack said, "what d'ya think of them fancy britches?"

"Quite a dandy, I'd say," Heck muttered around the lump of chaw.

Hickok smiled but cut his eyes to the two men on the porch who slowly put down their cards. One of the men was quietly easing a rifle onto his lap. The other had his right hand resting on his revolver.

With practiced nonchalance Hickok swung out of the saddle and stood facing Jack Chambers. Hickok figured he would have no problem outdrawing Jack. The other one—Heck—looked too stupid to be dangerous. But the two on the porch were a different story. Putting Nell between himself and those two blocked their view of his holster. And if Hickok did have to draw, he would have the critical extra few seconds he would need. Nell seemed to know what Hickok was up to. She stood as tall and rigid as a statue.

"I'm here on business," Hickok said calmly.

Heck Chambers walked up to Hickok with a mouthful of tobacco. Hickok frowned as Heck wiped away a dribble of juice that rolled down his chin. Heck looked intently into Hickok's face, then turned to his brother.

"Dang, Jack, is that a nose on his face or a duckbill?"

The men set to laughing. Hickok smiled good-naturedly.

"I believe you boys have something that belongs to the Overland Express Company."

The foolish grin slid from Heck Chambers's face.

"Is that a fact," he said.

"That's a fact," Hickok answered.

Heck Chambers kept his eye on Hickok as he called over his shoulder.

"Jack, this Mister Fancy Pants claims we got something of his."

"That's what the feller says, Heck," Jack Chambers called out in a mocking tone.

Heck let fly a stream of tobacco juice that landed with a splat on the toe of Hickok's boot. "Now what have you got to say, Mister Duckbill?"

"Like I said before," Hickok said. "You got a horse in that corral that belongs to the Overland Express Company. And I ain't leaving till I get it back."

Jack Chambers took a few steps forward. He was close enough that Hickok could smell the liquor on his breath.

"Listen here," Chambers said angrily. "I done had just about enough of you and your smart mouth. Now my advice to you is get back on this here horse and ride out of here before someone gets hurt—that someone being you!"

Hickok smiled. "Maybe you boys are hard of hearing," he said. "I told you I want my horse back."

Jack Chambers set his hands on his hips and shook his head.

"You're either the craziest man alive or the bravest, I'll admit." He rubbed his chin. "Okay, Mister Duckbill," Jack Chambers said, "I'll play along with your little game. Now what makes you think I stole your horse?"

"You're horse thieves, ain't you?" Hickok said.

Jack Chambers looked offended. "Horse thieves?" he repeated innocently. "No sir," he said, shaking his head. He jerked his head toward the corral behind him. "These here horses we found fair and square. And we aim to sell them to horse traders down south."

"That's right," his brother said. "We're legitimate businessmen. If you don't believe us, ask the constable. He'll tell you."

Hickok pulled down on the edges of his mustache. He stared past Jack Chambers to the corral. "I already done talked to the constable," Hickok said. "Claims I got no proof." Hickok took a step in the direction of the corral. Jack Chambers stepped sideways and blocked his way. He put his left hand against Hickok's chest, and the other hand went to his gun.

"Where you off to?" he snarled.

"To find my proof," Hickok said, pointing to the corral. "You got a pony express horse in there and I aim to prove it."

"Take one step," Chambers threatened, "and it'll be your last!" He backed up a few paces and set his feet apart in the familiar gunfighter's stance.

Jack Chambers reached for his gun. In a flash Hickok whipped out his pistol and fired. The gun flew from Chambers's hand. Flustered, Heck Chambers made a sudden clumsy reach for his gun.

"One move and I drop him," Hickok warned. Heck had the gun half out of his holster. He looked plaintively to his brother.

Jack Chambers snarled. "Do what he says, Heck!"

Heck dropped his pistol to the ground.

"Have those other boys drop their irons, too," Hickok ordered.

Chambers looked at the two men on the porch and nodded. They gingerly tossed their guns to the ground. A hint of a smile played on Hickok's face.

"Fetch the horse," Hickok called out to one of the men on the porch. He didn't move.

Jack Chambers licked his dry lips. "Do as he says, Buck. Bring the bay."

Buck jogged to the corral and led the horse to where Hickok stood.

Hickok smiled when he saw the pony express brand on the horse's flank.

"I guess this here's my proof." With his gun still pointing at Chambers, Hickok took the reins of the pony and swung up into the saddle. Nell whinnied.

"You ain't going to get away with this!" Chambers said. "I own this town." Hatred brimmed in his eyes. "I'll get you. I promise you that!"

Hickok calmly slipped the gun into his sash and looked down hard at Chambers.

"Everybody around here seems to have nothing but advice," Hickok said. "Well let me give you a little of my own." He leaned down so his words could be heard clear and simple. "Don't make promises you can't keep."

CHAPTER 4

Luke pressed Hickok for details of his confrontation with Jack Chambers.

"So how many were there?" he asked excitedly. "Was Chambers as mean and ornery as they say? Did you pull your gun?"

To Luke's everlasting disappointment, Hickok said little except that Jack Chambers had been "persuaded" to return the stolen horse.

"Ah, shoot," Luke muttered, kicking at the dirt with his boot.

It was a hot afternoon, and Hickok was sitting in a chair in the shade by the station house. He had brought out a stool and was cleaning his pistols with a rag. Luke had finished his chores and stood by and watched. Cody walked out from the station house. A bedroll was slung over his shoulder.

He walked over to where Hickok was sitting.

"Where are you going, Mr. Cody?" Luke asked. Hickok looked up from his polishing.

"I reckon it's about time I head back," Cody said.

"Luke," Hickok said, "go see to Mr. Cody's horse."
Luke ran to the corral to fetch the bay.

"Much obliged, Luke," Cody said as he took the reins from Luke. He swung up into the saddle and folded his arms casually over the horn.

Hickok put down his cleaning rag and leaned back in his chair. "You reckon you might be able to stay put in that saddle this time?" he asked Cody.

Cody pretended a look of exasperation as he slipped off his hat and ran his fingers back through his hair. "Now, you ain't going to start up on me about that *again,* are you?" He gave Hickok a playful smile as he pulled his hat down snugly on his head. Then he shook his head and sighed tragically.

"What's the matter, Mr. Cody?" Luke asked.

Cody looked at him and rubbed the back of his neck. "Well, Luke, I was just thinkin' on how those Chambers fellers come out of nowhere and jumped me like a bunch of snakes." Cody waved a hand in the air as if painting a picture for Luke. "There was at least a dozen of 'em, Luke," he began gravely. "And they came sneaking up on me from behind a bunch of rocks as cool and calm as an April breeze."

Luke was confused. "I thought you said they came riding at you out in the open like thunder from out of the sky?" Luke asked innocently. "You said they had their guns drawn and that bullets were whizzing by your head like raindrops made out of lead and—"

"Hold on there, Luke," Cody said. "Did I say it was the Chambers gang that jumped me?"

"Yes, sir, you did."

"Well, what I meant to say was that it weren't the Chambers gang at all."

"It wasn't?" Luke asked. Cody shook his head.

"What I'm thinkin' on was an entirely different incident," he said. "It was something that happened to me a few months back when I was on my way out of the Marysville station with a fresh horse and a loaded mochila."

"What happened?" Luke asked breathlessly.

"I do declare!" said Hickok, leaning forward in his chair and pointing at the ground. "It's a fact that the grass under that there horse you're on has grown two feet since you been in the saddle." A grin twisted up the corners of his mustache. He looked up at Cody. "What do you reckon might account for that?" he asked innocently.

Cody smiled and turned up his hands. "Fair enough," he said. "I give up." Cody turned to Luke and leaned down. "We'll continue this story next time I come through, Luke," he whispered.

"Now don't be riding off on my account," Hickok called out.

Cody laughed. "You know something, Hickok, you're just as ornery as ever. But it was a pleasure meeting up with you, anyway." From his saddle he bowed, sweeping his hands in front of him.

Hickok gave a quick wave. "The pleasure was all mine, Mr. Cody."

"And it was nice meeting you, Luke," Cody told the boy. Luke smiled as they shook hands. Cody gave a quick jerk to the reins. The bay did a quick turn and broke into a gallop. Luke ran down the road and waved. Luke watched Cody ride away, his back straight, his buckskin fringe and brown hair floating in the breeze.

Standing in the middle of the road, Luke sighed. The fact was, he thought to himself, William Cody wasn't too much older than he was. But while Bill Cody was having one real-life adventure after another, Luke had to settle for secondhand excitement from dime novels. Still, being able to actually meet and talk with men such as James Hickok and William Cody *was* exciting.

Luke walked back to where Hickok sat polishing his pistols.

"Ain't he grand?" Luke said.

Hickok turned to look out at the road, then looked down again. "Talks too much," Hickok said, "but he's all right."

Luke was eyeing the dismantled pistol on the stool in front of Hickok. He liked to watch Hickok clean his pistols. His hands worked smoothly and efficiently.

"One day I'm going to get me a set of pistols just like those," Luke said.

Hickok smiled as he picked up the disassembled barrel and squinted down its length. The rag he used to rub it down was dark with oil.

"I'm going to be the fastest draw in the territory one day," Luke boasted. "Then I won't be afraid of anybody."

Hickok lay down the barrel of the pistol. "It ain't knowing how to shoot a gun that earns a man respect," Hickok said.

Luke shrugged. "You mind if I hold your pistol?" he asked.

Hickok hesitated, then picked up the unloaded pistol and handed it to Luke, butt forward.

"Boy," Luke said, "it sure is heavy."

"It has to be heavy," Hickok said. "A pistol ain't much different than a cannon a man holds in his hands." His legs were apart, and his elbows rested on his knees. He was jamming the cloth down each chamber of the cylinder. He watched calmly as Luke palmed the pistol, testing its weight. Luke was sticking his tongue out from the effort.

Luke tried to cock the hammer with his thumb the way he had read about in his books.

"Use your whole thumb joint on the hammer," Hickok told him, "not just the tip of your thumb."

"This is awful hard," Luke said. The pistol was huge in his hand, and he needed his other to steady it as he tried to pull back the hammer.

"Some men file the hammer down till the trigger almost pulls itself," Hickok said. "But my thumbs are fast enough without such 'sweetening.' An easily tripped trigger is dangerous."

Luke examined the polished handles. "Where are the notches?" he asked. Gunfighters in his dime novels carved a notch in the handle of their gun, one for each man they killed. "Can you fan your gun?" Luke explained to Hickok how Deadeye Dick often rapidly fired his gun by holding down the trigger and slapping the hammer repeatedly with the palm of his hand.

Hickok scowled. "Fanning is for show-offs," he said bluntly, "and so are notches. Showing off can work for you, but most often it will work against you," Hickok explained. "A tough reputation can give you an edge in a duel. Some shootists tell outrageous lies about themselves. But sooner or later you'll be called upon to defend such a reputation." He gave Luke a sobering look. "That's no way for a man to live."

"You ever killed a man?" Luke asked. "Deadeye Dick has killed nearly a hundred!"

Hickok whistled. "Is that a fact?" he asked.

"I reckon so," Luke answered. "Well, did you?"

"Did I what?"

Luke dropped both his hands to his sides. "Did you ever kill a man?" he repeated.

Hickok put down his rag and took in a deep breath. His voice was almost a whisper. "One or two," he said. Hickok picked up the shiny clean cylinder, slid it into place, swung the barrel into position, and clicked it shut.

"Boy," said Luke, "I sure wish I was old enough to have me my own guns. Then I'd go after outlaws like Jack Chambers and his gang of rebel raiders. Why, I'd blast them for sure!" Luke dropped into his favorite gunfighter stance that he had seen illustrated in his dime novels. He hoisted the pistol up and pointed it at Hickok.

"BLAM! BLAM! BLAM!"

Hickok jumped from his chair like he was shot from a cannon. He grabbed the pistol from Luke and cursed. Luke was so startled by his sudden burst of anger that he stumbled backward and fell onto the ground. Hickok loomed over him. His eyes had gone to pure fury.

"Never point a gun at a man like that again!" Hickok shouted.

Luke burst into tears. "I was only fooling," he blubbered, swiping at his eyes with his shirtsleeve. "The gun ain't even loaded."

"It don't matter whether it's loaded or not, Luke. Just don't ever do it."

Luke's throat had tightened up, and he could hardly speak. "No sir, I won't," he managed to mutter.

Hickok stood for a minute staring at the pistol in his hand, then turned and laid it down gently on the stool. He sat down again, and his arms hung heavily at his sides. He finally put the heels of both hands to his fore- head and rubbed.

Luke sat up and wiped his eyes dry. He pulled his knees to his chest. He looked down at the ground, un- able to look Hickok in the eye.

"I want you to listen to me, Luke," he said kindly. Hickok leaned forward and reached out with his hand. He took the boy's chin in his fingers and tilted his face up so their eyes met. "It ain't like I take any pleasure from scolding you. But you have to be made to under- stand that a gun ain't never a toy."

Luke felt embarrassed. "I was just pretending," he muttered, "like in my books."

"I know it," Hickok said. "And there ain't no harm in reading about things in books. But books is one thing, and real life is another. In real life there ain't nothin' about guns or gunfighting to grin about. The decision to shoot a man is the most serious thinkin' a man can do. Once that decision is made, it can't ever be undone."

"I understand," Luke said. "I'm sorry."

"If I'm hard on you sometimes, Luke," Hickok said, "it's only because I want you to learn proper. And what you need to learn right now is that there's a whole lot more to guns than pulling a trigger." Hickok tapped the side of his head with his finger. "The best weapon a man has is his wits, son. That's the only weapon that will never fail a man. Remember that."

"I will," said Luke.

Hickok tried to coax a grin from Luke.

"That's more like it," he said as a crooked smile came to Luke's face. Reaching back to the stool, Hickok picked up the oily rag and held it out to Luke. "Blow that nose of yours into this," he told Luke.

Luke blew hard into the rag.

"Well," Hickok said, staring into the rag, "I guess I won't be cleaning anything else with this!"

Hickok laughed and stood up. Luke laughed, too.

"Luke, why don't you help me carry this back into the station house. It'll be suppertime soon enough."

Luke helped Hickok collect his gear. He was already feeling much better. "I reckon things will be a bit quieter now that Mr. Cody has rode off," Luke said as they climbed up the steps to the station house.

Hickok held the door open for Luke. "It'll be as quiet as a church at midnight," Hickok said.

Not long after that there was a knock on the station-house door. Then came the familiar voice of Parson Harte. "Afternoon, Luke!" he said, swatting his dusty hat against his thigh. Hickok stood up to shake his hand.

"Pleased to make your acquaintance, Reverend."

"And I yours, Mr. Hickok." The old man turned to Luke and smiled. "My grandson here can't stop talking about you, Mr. Hickok. The way Luke tells it you're just about the most famous man ever to set foot in Fairbury!" Luke turned crimson with embarrassment. The parson brought his hand down on the boy's shoulder and gave it a friendly shove.

"Shoot," Luke admitted shyly. "I ain't said *that* much."

Hickok and Parson Harte laughed.

"Famous or not, Mr. Hickok," Parson Harte said, "it would be my honor to have you to supper at our home at your earliest convenience. You're new to Fairbury, and I thought a home-cooked meal might be a pleasant change of pace from station-house food."

Luke's eyes went wide with anticipation. "What d'ya say, Mr. Hickok? Will you come? Will you?"

Hickok threw up both hands in mock surrender. He tipped his head in thanks.

"Reverend, I'd be honored."

CHAPTER 5

All day Luke had been jumpy with anticipation. More than once that early evening Parson Harte had had to scold Luke for staring out the window.

"Land's sake, Luke!" the old man teased. "If Mr. Hickok comes up that road and sees you staring bug-eyed out that window like some startled jackrabbit, he's likely to turn right around and head for home."

"I just can't sit still, Grandpa," Luke complained. "It's like I got bugs in my britches." Luke gave a mournful sound as he plunked himself down in a chair. Parson Harte smiled.

"Don't you worry, Luke. He'll be here."

"You sure, Grandpa?" said Luke fretfully.

Parson Harte shook his head when, for what seemed the millionth time, Luke dragged himself to the window.

"I see him!" Luke shouted finally. "He's here!"

"Well, I tried to tell you, boy," the old man said as he dried his hands on an apron.

Luke ran outside to greet Hickok.

"Evening, Luke," Hickok said with a modest tip of his hat. "Reverend."

Parson Harte and Hickok shook hands.

"Welcome to our home, Mr. Hickok," he said. "I hope you're hungry."

Hickok smiled shyly. "I expect I could eat a bite or two."

"That's fine," Parson Harte said. "C'mon in and make yourself comfortable."

All through supper Luke stared at Hickok in open-mouthed admiration. Everything Hickok said, no matter how trivial, filled Luke with wonder and excitement. Hickok did the best he could to ignore Luke's awe by concentrating on two helpings of pot roast, beans, hot biscuits, mashed potatoes, gravy, and peach pie.

"Tell us about the time you was attacked by a grizzly bear!" Luke asked Hickok excitedly.

"Good heavens," his grandfather said, "let the poor man swallow his food."

"Oh, I don't mind none," Hickok said finally. It had been a long time since Hickok had had such a fine meal, and he was feeling rather talkative.

"First off, Luke," he said, "it wasn't a grizzly that attacked me. It was a cinnamon bear. But plenty mean all the same."

"What happened?" Luke asked breathlessly. He was leaning forward, and his chin was resting in the cradle of his palms.

"One day I'm minding my own business when I

come across this bear down by a creek. Don't rightly know what riled her, but all of a sudden she's on me tight as a tick on a hound dog! I swung my rifle up right quick and fired off two shots." Hickok had his arms raised as if to shoot. *"BLAM! BLAM!"*

Luke nearly hopped right out of his seat.

Hickok shook his head.

"That bear's skull was so hard those two bullets skipped right off like a stone over pond water!"

He took a long sip of his coffee. "That dang crazy she-bear took a couple of swipes at me and nearly tore my arm right off." He turned his face to the light of the kerosene lamp. "She done put this here crease in my neck, too."

"Gosh," said Luke. "What happened then?"

"We tangled something awful, that's for sure."

Luke waited with eyes wide for Hickok to finish, but he seemed lost in thought. Finally, Parson Harte pushed himself up from his chair and walked to the stove. That must have been an awfully mean bear to give him that scar, Luke decided. He was anxious to find out what happened next, but the glance his grandfather gave him dissuaded him.

"More coffee, Mr. Hickok?" Parson Harte asked, politely changing the topic.

Hickok roused himself and nodded. "Thank you, Reverend," he said quietly.

"So, Mr. Hickok," the old man said as he sat down again. "Do you have family?"

"I have two sisters and two brothers back in Homer, Illinois," he said. "And one brother, Oliver, lives all the way out in California."

"I'd sure like a brother," Luke said wistfully.

"When did you leave home?"

"In fifty-six," Hickok said. "Came west with my brother, Lorenzo, to buy farmland for the family. My mother took sick, and Lorenzo went home to care for her."

"But you stayed?" Luke said.

"The fact is I got myself tangled up in the Kansas-Missouri border war. My father was an abolitionist. He taught me that no man has the right to make another man a slave—no matter what his skin color."

Parson Harte nodded his approval.

"Anyway, for a time I rode with General James Lanes's Free State Army. After that I spent some time as a constable in Monticello in Johnson County. But I was only twenty-one, and since I had hopes of reaching twenty-two I figured I'd best retire from the law-enforcement business."

"This is a lawless territory," Parson Harte said. "We could do with a man such as yourself. Bring some law and order to town. Teach folks they don't have to be scared just because some men carry a gun."

"You'd be talking about Jack Chambers and his bunch."

Parson Harte nodded. "And that good-for-nothing constable. Why, he's no better than a hired gun for Chambers. Does whatever Chambers says."

"Why don't folks stand up to him?" Hickok asked.

Parson Harte took a deep breath and sighed. "Mr. Hickok, I've been preaching that very message for years, but it doesn't seem to do any good." He turned his hands palm up. "Chambers has this town so bullied that no one can think himself straight."

"I never could abide a bully," Hickok said. "Once, when I was a boy, my brother and I went swimming with some other boys in Tomahawk Creek. There was this one feller—can't remember his name—but he was dunking all the smaller boys who couldn't swim. Next thing you know this one boy was swept out and came darn near close to drowning."

"What did you do?" Luke asked.

"I jumped in and pulled him out. But when I got to shore I saw that skunk of a bully sneakin' off. So's I picked him up and flung him in the creek!"

At that they all laughed.

After a few more stories Hickok pulled a watch from his trousers and said it was getting late. The moon was already up in the east.

Before Hickok said good night, Parson Harte asked him to wait while he rummaged in the other room.

"I want you to have this," he said, offering Hickok a gilt-edged, leather-bound Bible.

Hickok nodded gravely. "Much obliged."

Later that night Luke stared up at the ceiling in his room. Thinking about James Hickok, Luke decided he was done with Deadeye Dick forever. No dime-novel hero could compare with the real thing.

CHAPTER 6

The next evening Hickok sat in the Calico Cat, Fairbury's approximation of a saloon. It was a combination town hall, church, and watering hole. Mostly it was a place for folks from town to meet and socialize.

In the corner Rufus, the piano player, sat hunched over his keys.

A familiar argument had broken out among the men gathered at some tables near the makeshift bar.

"What is it with this Lincoln feller, anyway?" griped old farmer Silas. "I'd never even heard of him, and all of a sudden he's president of the United States and war breaks out!"

"Didn't you read those old newspaper accounts of his debate against Stephen Douglas?" a young farmer named Red John asked. "He was a congressman from Illinois, and he come right out against the spread of slavery."

"What does he plan to do with all the Negroes if they're ever set free?" Old Silas asked.

Red John stroked a stubbled chin. "Don't rightly know," he said. "Just said he wouldn't give 'em the vote."

A ranch hand named Smithers fretted. "If they do set the slaves free, we'll all lose our jobs!" There was mumbled agreement from some men. "I won't work as cheap as a freed colored man."

Hickok tried to concentrate on the poker hand before him. He looked around the table at the other poker players. Even the dealer had an attentive ear cocked in the direction of the bar where the men argued.

Thomas Green, the poker player on Hickok's right, objected.

"How can you outlaw slavery?" he said. "The Constitution guarantees each state's right to choose! I say each state should have the right to decide on its own whether it wants slavery or not."

"Popular sovereignty has brought nothing but trouble to the territories," Dr. Day argued.

"The real problem isn't slavery," said the shopkeeper, Mr. Reising. "It's economics."

Red John laughed. "You mean, like running a store? You've been working too hard, Mr. Reising."

The shopkeeper smoothed his trousers with his hands. "Ever since the cotton gin speeded cotton production, the South has been making lots of money selling raw cotton to French and English mills."

"What's that got to do with anything?" Red John demanded impatiently.

Mr. Reising answered. "The government has been using the proceeds from Southern tax money to help build factories and mills up North. Now Northern politicians are demanding that the South sell its cotton only to them even though France and England are willing to pay higher prices." He smiled smoothly. "Why, that would be like me saying you had to sell your corn to me even if you could get a higher price from another store."

The young farmer frowned. "I wouldn't stand for that."

"Neither has the South," Mr. Reising said. "But the law is on the side of the North, because there are more Northerners in Congress. Taxation without representation started the American Revolution, and it has started another war."

Parson Harte whisked closed the newspaper he was reading and jumped to his feet. His eyes were alive with passion.

"How can you say the conflict is not about slavery?" he demanded.

"Quite simply," answered Mr. Reising calmly. "Just four years ago the Supreme Court ruled in its Dred Scott decision that Congress does not have the right to restrict slavery in the territories."

"That's right!" another man joined in. "The chief justice himself said slaves have no rights that white men are bound by law to respect."

Parson Harte shook his head sadly. "It was a pitiful decision," he said.

"That's your opinion, Reverend," said Mr. Reising.

The old man was not through. "This evil called slavery has pulled this country apart. Why, right here in Fairbury neighbors are willing to kill one another over it." A few months back an argument between two men

about slavery had so infuriated one of them that he had recklessly pulled a gun on the other.

The man, Stevenson, fired on his friend. The other man, a young farmer, died a few days later.

The parson turned to appeal to the other men. "Gentlemen, it is not each other we should be fighting, but the lawlessness that this evil has engendered."

There was some confused grumbling and here and there a murmur of approval.

"What exactly are you saying, Parson?" a farmer named Hastings asked.

"I'm saying," he replied patiently, "that it is men like Jack Chambers we should be fighting and not one another." Parson Harte looked from one man to the next. "Don't you see, we'll never have any peace in this town as long as we allow people like Jack Chambers to run things."

"How do you expect me to stand up to Jack Chambers?" Silas said. "He'd cut me down sooner than I could blink."

"That's right!" came a shout from the back.

"He's right!" came another voice.

Just then there was a commotion by the open door of the hall. The room fell silent. Rufus's hands stopped over the piano keys, his last chord fading in the air like a cloud of frozen breath. All eyes turned to the man in the tan duster.

"What's the matter, folks," said Jack Chambers. "Cat got your tongue?" Chambers walked up to Parson Harte and flipped open his duster. He pushed back his hat and shook his head.

"Listen here, old man. Word around town has it that you've got some mighty unflattering things to say about me. A lot of lies from what I can tell."

Parson Harte looked Chambers straight in the eye. "I only tell the truth."

"What did you say, old man?" Chambers asked with a sneer of disbelief.

"What's the matter, Jack?" shouted Hickok from the back of the room. "You still got bad ears?" Chambers spun around with his gun drawn.

The crowd peeled back in a frightened panic.

Chambers's eyes went dark and mean. "You!" he said.

Hickok smiled and nonchalantly crossed his legs at the ankles. He folded his arms across his chest.

Chambers marched right up to him. His boot heels echoed dully on the plank floor. Hickok recognized one of Chambers's men standing near the door. He guessed it was the one Luke called Cockeyed Frank.

"You and I have some unfinished business, Duckbill," Chambers said.

Hickok smoothed out his cards on the table. "That was settled," he said quietly.

Chambers shook his head. "Not to my satisfaction," he growled.

"Please, Mr. Chambers!" Ruben, the bartender, begged. "Don't shoot the place up! I'm still paying for the mirror you broke last time."

Chambers sneered, pulled his gun, and fired. The mirror exploded in a shower of tinkling glass. Chambers swung around and pointed his pistol at Hickok. Hickok

was pinned behind the table—not the best position from which to defend oneself.

Hickok whistled. For a second Chambers was bewildered. Then there was an explosion as Nell crashed into the bar. Chairs flew left and right as astonished patrons dove for cover.

Nell swung her hindquarters around, and Chambers tripped over his own boots trying to get out of her way. Hickok saw Cockeyed Frank reach for his gun. Hickok waved his hand overhead as a warning, and Nell obediently fell to the floor. Frank's shot whizzed over her head. Just as quickly Nell was up again.

Hickok leapt on Nell's back, and in a flash they flew out of the barroom.

Chambers scrambled to his feet. "I'll get you, Duckbill!" he roared after them.

The saloon had emptied out except for Jack Chambers and Cockeyed Frank. Chambers kicked at an overturned chair. Obviously Hickok was smarter than he had thought. What he needed, he realized, was the proper net to snare him. He thought for a minute and then turned to Cockeyed Frank.

"Ain't Hickok friendly with that parson and his grandkid?" Chambers asked.

Cockeyed Frank shrugged and rubbed his cheek. "Yeah, I reckon. Why?"

A malicious grin slowly came over Jack Chambers's face. "Maybe it's time someone taught that meddlin' old abolitionist fool a lesson."

CHAPTER 7

Hickok expected trouble from the Chambers gang all week. But to his surprise the trouble did not come.

Nine o'clock that Sunday morning Hickok settled down in one of the rickety chairs lined up in neat rows in the saloon. Ruben had hung a tablecloth over the painting of a nude woman that usually overlooked the room from the bar. Another cloth covered the rows of liquor bottles beneath the shattered mirror. A sign declared: The Bar Is Closed Until 1 P.M.

Hickok carefully smoothed the long tails of his black frock coat and adjusted the watch chain crossing his embroidered silk vest. All around him sat the freshly scrubbed townsfolk in their Sunday best. The men had their hair slicked down with scented oil. The ladies wore neatly ironed calico dresses and their finest bonnets and hats.

Hickok barely recognized Red John out of his muddy overalls. Even Old Silas looked like he'd shaken hands with a bar of soap.

"Mornin', Mr. Duckbill," Silas cackled. His laughter stuck in his skinny old neck when he saw Hickok's eyes frost over like a pond in February.

"Sorry, just funnin'," Silas mumbled.

The murmur of gossip and greetings quickly hushed when Parson Harte stepped up to the portable pulpit. He pulled himself up to his full height and gripped his lapels with his fists. His eyes solemnly surveyed the congregation. Someone suppressed a cough.

"All rise and turn to page five in your hymn books," Harte began. "Let us sing."

Chairs scraped and there was a ruffling of pages as the congregation rose to its feet. Hickok was startled straight up in his seat when Rufus banged out the opening chords of a rousing hymn.

I couldn't do any more damage if I pounded on those keys with a hammer, Hickok told himself.

A woman with a voice like a rusty hinge led the hymn. Hickok winced through all three verses, then, when the song finally ended, said a grateful "Amen."

Once the congregation was seated, Parson Harte cleared his throat. "I would like to begin today's sermon with a quote from the great Negro orator Frederick Douglass: 'There is not a man beneath the canopy of heaven that does not know that slavery is wrong for him.'"

"Amen!" someone shouted.

Parson Harte took a deep breath. "If we know slavery is wrong for us," he thundered, "how can we not also know that it is wrong for every other human being? Do unto others as you would have others do unto you!"

Murmurs of assent droned and buzzed through the assembly.

Mr. Harte went on gravely. "Would *you* be made a slave? Would you be branded like cattle? Would you be chained? Would you be torn from your loved ones and sold like horseflesh?"

Hickok had to admit that the old man was an impassioned and persuasive orator. Even so, the heat from the crowded room and the lulling rhythms of the parson's rumbling voice were rocking Hickok to sleep.

At a particularly passionate passage in the sermon, Hickok jerked to attention. "Some people argue that Negroes are nothing more than animals," Parson Harte roared, "and therefore it is not wrong to treat them as such. But I ask you, can an animal speak and learn to read? Can an animal cry for that which has gone by or worry about what might occur in the future? Does an animal have an immortal soul?"

Suddenly Jack Chambers burst into the hall. Light flooded in through the open doors.

"You better pray for yours, old man!" he shouted from the doorway.

The stunned congregation turned as one toward the door of the saloon. Jack Chambers was leading his gang into the Calico Cat. Their guns were drawn.

Well, well, Hickok thought, here comes trouble.

Hickok reached for his Navy Colts.

"Just try it, Duckbill," Chambers purred. As if Hickok were a magnet, the gang's guns were extended toward him.

"Sit down," Jack Chambers ordered Hickok. He turned to one of his gang. "And Frank, if this fancy pants so much as blinks, shoot him."

Cockeyed Frank smiled. "With pleasure, Jack."

Chambers grabbed Parson Harte. "I done told you before, old man. I'm sick and tired of you inciting folks against slavery and dragging my good name through the gutter. All this abolitionist talk and name-calling is bad for business." He waved his gun at the congregation. "In fact," he said, "I'm just plain tired of hearing you!" He began to drag the preacher away. "Sermon's over, folks!" he said. "The reverend here is coming for a little ride with us."

Luke rushed out from the crowd. "Let him go!" he shouted. Jack Chambers flung Luke roughly to the floor. His eyes had gone cold and dark. "Now, any of you other yellowbellies got anything to add?"

No one said a word.

"I'll be all right, son," Parson Harte told Luke.

Jack Chambers snorted sarcastically. "Sure he'll be all right. He'll be joining the angels in heaven."

Heck Chambers swung a noose like a lariat. "Yup," he said. "Your grandpappy will be climbing this here ladder to the pearly gates."

When Chambers and his gang left, Hickok jumped to his feet and spun the cylinders of both his pistols.

There was a murmur from the congregation and some nervous shuffling.

"You aim to go after him?" someone asked Hickok.

Hickok looked at the man with disbelief. "Well I sure ain't going to stand by and do nothing!"

"Maybe someone should call the constable."

Hickok scowled. "You couldn't get that no-account constable out of his chair with a stick of dynamite. We'll have to go after Chambers and his boys ourselves." Hickok straightened his hat and settled his pistols comfortably in his sash. "Now, who's with me?"

One by one the men slunk away or dropped their eyes to the floor.

The silence was deafening.

"I'm with you, Mr. Hickok!" came a lone voice from a corner of the room.

The crowd stared in amazement. Hickok smiled at Luke.

"That's brave of you, Luke. But I'm afraid this here's a man's job." He looked disgustedly around the room. "And I reckon there just ain't no men to be found *here*. Nothin' here but a bunch of frightened sheep."

Without another word Hickok raced out the door.

CHAPTER 8

BLAM! BLAM!

Shots rang out the instant Hickok hit the street in front of the saloon. He dove to the ground just as two bullets whizzed by his ear.

"Dang!" Hickok muttered into the dirt. "He's getting away." He watched helplessly as the wagon with Chambers and Parson Harte thundered down the street toward the edge of town.

Hickok looked left and right but couldn't see any sign of Nell or any other horse. Must have scattered the horses, Hickok thought. Still on his stomach, he crawled behind the shelter of a watering trough. Some of Chambers's men might have hung back just in case anyone decided to ride out after them.

"Sure wish I knew where Nell was," Hickok wondered aloud. He gave a whistle, and suddenly from around a deserted street corner Nell appeared. "That a girl!" Hickok beamed. He waved his hat, and instantly Nell broke into a gallop. Hickok came out from behind his hiding place and waited in the street until Nell passed by. In one elegant motion Hickok grabbed the saddle horn and swung himself up into the saddle.

"It's just you and me, Nell!" Hickok said as he patted her affectionately on the neck. Nell shook her head and raced toward the edge of town.

Hickok caught Chambers's trail not far out from town. He pulled on the reins and brought Nell to a stop on a tree-shaded rise above a creek. Hickok leaned his arms over the saddle horn and peered through the trees. He could see the wagon in the distance. Parson Harte was standing in the wagon bed. His hands appeared to be tied at the wrists. Someone—it looked like Heck Chambers—was slipping a rope around the old man's neck.

Nell pawed nervously at the dirt.

Hickok pushed back the brim of his hat. "I know what you mean, girl," he said. "It's right suspicious Chambers stopping that wagon so far out in the open and all. If I didn't know better, I'd think this was some kind of trap."

Hickok gave a whistle, and Nell began a slow trot toward the wagon. If it was a trap, and Hickok was certain that it was, it would be best not to rush in with guns blazing.

Jack Chambers smirked when he caught sight of Hickok.

"Thought you'd show up, Duckbill," he said. "Come any closer and I send the team running!"

Heck Chambers tightened the noose around the parson's neck. He looped the other end over a high, stout tree branch, then tied it to the tree trunk.

Hickok studied the rope. It was too thick to sever with one shot, and he doubted he'd have a chance at two.

"Just wait your turn, Duckbill," Jack Chambers smiled. "Unless you'd rather go first."

"Save yourself!" Harte shouted.

Heck Chambers laughed. "Maybe we should string them both up at once. There's more rope in the wagon."

"Enough for all of us?" called a voice from behind Hickok, back up on the rise. It was Mr. Reising!

The gang had been too busy taunting Hickok to notice that the entire congregation had followed Hickok to the creek!

Seeing themselves outnumbered, two of Chambers's men wheeled their horses and rode away as fast as they could. "Come back here, you yellow dogs!" Jack Chambers roared.

Luke rushed to his grandfather and lifted the noose from over his head. He hugged the old man hard.

Jack Chambers looked coldly from the preacher to the crowd. Constable Lee sat on a big, dappled gray at the edge of the gathering. Both horse and rider were puffing and out of breath.

"Aren't you going to arrest them?" Red John demanded.

"What for?" Constable Lee asked. "Interrupting a sermon?"

"Attempted murder!" Mr. Reising cried indignantly.

"Now, now. This is nothing to get all riled up about. Just a misunderstanding. Isn't that right?" the constable asked Chambers.

"That's right," Chambers said. "No harm meant."

Lee turned to the crowd.

"Go on home, folks! The show's over." No one moved. "Go on! Or I'll arrest you all for disturbing the peace."

Jack Chambers and his men laughed. Heck Chambers doubled over and clutched his sides.

"Go on," Constable Lee commanded, puffing out his large stomach.

"You'll arrest us but not them?" Red John asked. "You're no lawman," he said disgustedly.

"I'd say it's time we held a new election," Mr. Reising shouted.

"I nominate Red John for constable," Old Silas yelled.

"All those in favor, raise your right hand," Mr. Reising called.

Every man except the members of the Chambers gang raised his right hand.

"I'd say it's unanimous," Silas crowed.

Mr. Reising took the badge from Lee and ceremoniously pinned the tin star to the young farmer's overalls.

Red John looked from the star to Jack Chambers. "You're under arrest."

Jack Chambers laughed. A cruel sneer twisted his face. He turned his horse and said, "C'mon, boys."

But a gunshot exploded, and Jack Chambers's hat

flew into the air. He stopped his horse and slowly turned in his saddle.

Hickok's steady hand held his Colt with the smoking muzzle pointing at Chambers's heart. "You do have the worst ears of any man I ever knowed!" Hickok said calmly. "The man said you're under arrest."

Jack Chambers shot Hickok a look of pure hatred. A malicious grin played at the corners of his mouth. "Only too happy to oblige," he drawled sarcastically. Then he turned to the crowd. "But when I get out—and I will—I'll remember who put me in jail. Each and every one of you!" He spoke in a low tone to Hickok.

"This ain't finished," he told Hickok. "I promise you that."

Hickok shrugged. "Last time we met you cost me a winning hand at poker. This time you interrupted my Sunday morning nap. You're starting to make me mad."

"It'll cost you a lot more than Sunday morning shut-eye if you don't get your hide out of my territory!"

Red John dragged Chambers down from his horse.

"From now on your territory is a jail cell," Red John said, tying a stout rope around Chambers's wrists.

Hickok helped disarm and tie up the other men. Silas whooped. "Let's go back to the Calico Cat and celebrate!"

The townsfolk rode off cheering, with Red John and his prisoners bringing up the rear.

CHAPTER 9

ickok was relieved when the steel door shut behind Jack Chambers and his gang.

"That oughtta keep you boys comfortable till the sheriff gets here," Red John said. A fast rider had been dispatched to the county seat. Red John sat in the constable's chair and put his big, muddy boots on the desk. He smiled.

"Don't take it too easy," Hickok said. "I count four in that cell. That leaves two on the loose."

Jack Chambers glared through the bars.

Red John dropped his feet to the floor. "You think they'll try to bust out these snakes?"

Hickok's hand strayed to his gun butts. Red John needed no other reply.

"I best figure on staying here tonight," Red John said.

Hickok nodded. "If you need to get home for a while, I can stand watch."

"Would you?" Red John asked gratefully. "I've got to get the cows in and feed the horses."

"I'll be here," Hickok agreed.

Red John returned a few hours later with a hamperful of supper.

"Are you sure you don't want me to stay?" Hickok offered.

The new constable shook his head. "Now's as good a time as any to start being constable. Mr. Reising said he'd come by around six to take a turn with me."

"It's nightfall you have to worry about," Hickok said.

"Don't worry, Mr. Hickok," Red John said. "I'll be careful."

Hickok had been invited to another supper with Luke and Parson Harte. It was about sundown when he arrived, and once again the parson had outdone himself.

This time they feasted on hickory ham and potatoes, buttered peas, biscuits, and the sweetest apple pie Hickok could ever remember tasting.

Pushing himself away from the table, Hickok gave his stomach a satisfying thump.

"If I'm not careful," he joked, "I'm liable to wind up like Bill Cody!"

"Oh?" Harte asked.

"A pony express rider," Hickok said, "who talks and eats more than anybody alive. It's a miracle he don't stab himself in the tongue!"

They all laughed.

"*I'd* like to be just like Bill Cody and ride for the pony express," Luke said dreamily.

Hickok smiled and nodded. He couldn't fault the boy for his dream. Being a pony express rider did have some glory to it, especially for a young boy growing up on dime-novel heroics. But Hickok knew that the pony express was an idea whose time had already come and gone. Telegraph wires were going up all over the country, and before long the pony express would be just a memory.

Hickok didn't want to think about that just now.

He took out his fiddle and happily obliged Luke and Parson Harte with an enthusiastic rendition of some familiar songs.

Before long Hickok noticed Luke's head bobbing up and down with sleep.

"I expect it's about time for me to shove off," Hickok said.

They said their good nights, and under a clear sky filled with thousands of blinking stars, Hickok rode with leisurely fatigue back to the station.

Just in sight of the station, however, Nell stopped. She bucked nervously. Hickok snapped alert and sensed instantly that something was wrong.

He had expected to see Clancy on the porch playing his harmonica and maybe a light where Jed liked to read. But the station appeared deserted.

The horses in the corral whinnied. Nell stamped and snorted. Hickok patted the mare's neck. He knew she could smell strangers, and he had a good idea who his "visitors" were.

Suddenly a light came up in the station house and the door swung open. A shadowy figure stepped out. Hickok knew immediately that it was Jack Chambers.

"Say your prayers, Duckbill!" Jack Chambers said. "Only heaven can save you now, Yankee!"

Hickok smiled, thinking he might reach for the Bible in his saddlebag, the Bible given to him by the parson. With all due respect to the reverend, Hickok thought, this time I'll reach for my Colt revolvers!

Heck joined his brother on the station-house porch. He laughed and swung a noose in a circle above his head. "It's your turn now."

"Where are my riders?" Hickok demanded.

"Trussed up like little piggies in here," Heck said.

"We don't care about those boys," Jack said. "It's you we're after, Duckbill."

Hickok figured the rest of the gang was lurking in the shadows.

Sure enough, Cockeyed Frank stepped out from the shadow of the barn. "Slide off that horse nice and easy," he said. He fired a warning shot over Hickok's head.

Hickok whipped the pistol from his sash, and he dropped Cockeyed Frank in a flash of fire and smoke.

Instantly there was an explosion like a string of fire-crackers as the rest of the gang burst out of hiding and opened fire.

Bullets ripped into the station's walls as Hickok dove off Nell and onto the hard ground. He landed hard on his still-tender left arm and winced. He crawled behind a large boulder. That, and the darkness, provided

Hickok with his only protection. His left arm throbbed. Bullets whizzed by in a rain of lead.

They're panicked, Hickok thought. That's why their shots are going wild.

Hickok bided his time and waited. He listened, mapping out their positions in his head. He sprang to his knees and fired four shots. Four men fell.

Hickok drew his second pistol. He heard boots stumping on the porch and the sound of the station-house door slamming shut.

A sudden silence settled with the dust. Hickok decided it was time to make his move before whoever was inside had a chance to reload.

Crouching low, he ran to the station-house door and turned his back to the wall.

"Give yourself up or I'm coming in after you!" Hickok yelled. Hickok kicked open the door with a crash.

THWACK!

A knife smacked into the doorjamb just inches from Hickok.

Against the back wall of the station house, Jack Chambers crouched behind an upturned table. Hickok coolly regarded the trembling knife blade and pulled it free of the wood. He tossed the knife back to Jack, then pulled his own knife from his sash.

Hickok stepped into the room. "You said we had some unfinished business. Let's finish it!"

Chambers jerked his bowie knife from the floorboards at his feet.

He roared like an angry bear and leapt at Hickok. Both men crashed to the floor. Hickok landed again on his painful left arm and the knife twisted from his grip.

Hickok jerked back and forth as Chambers slashed at Hickok with his knife. Hickok dove to his right and managed to grab his own knife.

"It's you or me, Yankee pig!" Chambers snarled through gritted teeth. "You're dead meat, and I'm the butcher."

Hickok shot his knife up and caught the other man's blade against the hilt. Then he twisted his wrist to wrench Chambers's blade and send it spinning across the floor.

Chambers's fist thwacked into Hickok's face. Hickok's head snapped back as Chambers scrambled for the knife.

Hickok struggled to raise himself to his knees. His head was reeling as if he were underwater. Through bleary eyes Hickok saw his enemy turn toward him. Chambers raised his knife over his head and lunged. With all his strength Hickok drove his bowie knife up. . . . Then he blacked out.

CHAPTER 10

It was Old Silas who found Red John that evening, bound and gagged in the jail cell where he'd tossed Jack Chambers and his men. "They went to the express station!" Red John shouted. He sprang for the door and was on his horse in seconds. "I'll need help," Red John shouted to Old Silas. "Round up a posse!" Old Silas did as he was told, and it seemed that half the town was already awake and mingling in the street by the time Red John galloped out to the station.

"What happened?" they asked Old Silas excitedly.

"The whole Chambers gang attacked Hickok at the pony express station!"

"Something like that was bound to happen after the way he showed those varmints up today," Mr. Green said.

"Six to one is awfully mean odds," said Mr. Reising.

"Well, let's even 'em up!" shouted a young ranch hand. "Go for your guns, boys!"

Parson Harte leaned out the door and shouted at the passing parade of men and horses. "What's all the ruckus?"

"Trouble at the express station!" Mr. Reising called out. "We're headed out there now."

Luke scooted around his grandfather and out the door.

"Hold on there, young man," the old man said. "Where do you think you're going?"

"Mr. Hickok's in trouble. I've got to help him," Luke yelled on his way to the barn.

When Luke reached the station, Constable Red John stood on the porch. He held up his hands for order. "It's all over, folks," he said. Luke pushed past the men crowding the station steps. Dr. Day stopped him at the door. "You don't want to go in there, son."

"But Mr. Hickok . . . ," Luke pleaded.

"Yes, Mr. Harte?" Hickok stepped from the station house.

"You're all right!" Luke cried.

"I was lucky," Hickok replied, ruffling Luke's hair. "The same can't be said for those other boys, though."

"Did you whup 'em all?" Old Silas called out in amazement.

"You won't have any more trouble from the Chambers gang," Hickok said modestly.

The townsfolk cheered and threw their hats in the air and shot their guns for joy.

"Hooray for Duckbill!" Old Silas yelled.

"*Wild* Bill is more like it!" Luke shouted.

Hickok stroked his chin. *Wild Bill* Hickok, he thought and smiled. Darned if I don't like the sound of that.

CHAPTER 11

Hickok was enjoying a final Sunday dinner with Luke and Parson Harte. It was a golden early evening, and a breeze, smelling of dust and prairie grass, blew in through an open window.

Hickok pushed away his plate and sighed contentedly. "Much obliged, Reverend."

Parson Harte nodded his head in thanks. "No trouble at all, Mr. Hickok."

Hickok smiled. "We've been friends for quite a spell now," he said. "Don't you think it's about time you dropped the *mister?*"

"You mean, we should call you Wild Bill?" Luke teased. A big grin played on his face.

Hickok sighed in mock weariness. He looked in appeal to Parson Harte.

The old man chuckled and turned up his hands. "Some things that stick just can't get unstuck."

Hickok looked at Luke and shrugged helplessly. He playfully shook his head in horror. "I just hope Bill Cody never hears about this!" he groaned.

He picked up his fiddle and idly plucked the strings. Ever since his confrontation with Jack Chambers and his gang, these regular Sunday dinners with Luke and Parson Harte had become a welcome ritual in Hickok's life. Sharing a home-cooked supper with Luke and his grandfather was the closest Hickok had come in a long time to having his own family. It was going to be hard to leave.

Hickok set the fiddle down. No one seemed much interested in music tonight.

It was Parson Harte who spoke first.

"We'll be forever in your debt," he told Hickok warmly.

Hickok shook his head, then winked at Luke. "I'm not the one who made this peach pie."

The old man smiled. "I meant the town," he amended. "For saving us from the Chambers gang."

"Shoot," Hickok said, and shrugged. If Luke didn't know better, he would have thought Hickok looked a trace embarrassed. Hickok picked up his fork and drummed it lightly along the edge of his plate. After a while, he spoke. "You saved yourselves," he said seriously. "Just by taking a stand."

Parson Harte nodded in agreement.

"Weren't you ever afraid?" Luke asked. "Not even when Jack Chambers and his rebel gang had you outnumbered?"

Hickok gave Luke's words a thoughtful pause. "I suppose it wouldn't be natural if a man didn't experience some fear sometimes," Hickok explained to the boy.

"But you can't let fear rule your life and keep you from doing what you know is right."

"Like joining up to fight the proslavery armies of the South?" Luke asked.

Hickok considered. "Maybe." He leaned back in his chair and stared toward the open window. Then he rolled his chair forward and gave Luke a thoughtful look. "The way I figure it is this, Luke," he said. "States in the South have decided that if they can't have slaves, they don't want to be part of these here United States anymore." He pulled on the edge of his mustache. "Now, I don't know whether the Constitution gives them the right to do that or not."

"You mean, can they secede from the Union?" Luke asked.

"That's a fancier word for it," Hickok said, "but it means the same thing. They say they have that right to secede. President Lincoln says they don't." He turned the palms of both hands upward. "I ain't a politician, Luke, and I don't have the schooling to answer a question like that." He pointed a long finger into the air. "But I'll tell you this." The finger curled to his chest. "In here, I know in my heart that no man has the right to keep another man a slave."

"You learned that from your daddy, didn't you?" Luke said.

Hickok smiled at the memory of his father. "That's right."

"Your father was a good man," said Parson Harte with approval. "Like his son."

Again Hickok squirmed with embarrassment. All the same, he thanked the parson. The old man pushed himself up from the table and asked Luke to help him clear the dishes.

He brought a pot of coffee and set it down.

"Thank you, Reverend." Hickok sipped at his coffee. The parson had his hands cradled around his cup and his eyes lowered as if something was on his mind. Without looking up, he said, "I'm not a sentimental man, Mr. Hickok." He looked up. "But I'll miss you." He turned to Luke. "And I know Luke will, too."

"I'm much obliged to you both," Hickok said with true warmth and affection.

"Are you sure you have to go?" Luke asked.

Hickok said that he did.

For a while they talked about the changes that had taken place in Fairbury since the Chambers gang was put in jail. Parson Harte shook his head. "I thought getting those thieving rascals out of town might solve our problems," he said in a tone both quiet and anxious, "but it looks like the trouble is only just beginning."

Hickok agreed and solemnly nodded his head.

"People say this war will be a short one," Parson Harte began gravely. "I think they're wrong. The armies of President Jefferson Davis and his Confederate states have the horses, guns, and ammunition they need to wage war against Lincoln and his federal troops. Armies of the South soon will march in bloody conflict against armies of the North. And why? Because some men believe it just and right to own men like cattle or dogs or sheep. It's intolerable!" The passion of the old man's antislavery sentiments was bringing a flush of indignation to his face. His fists were clenched, and he brought one hand down hard on the table.

"Slavery is a blight and an evil," he said. "Slavery is—"

"An *abomination!*" Luke chimed in.

A hint of a smile played at the corner of the old man's mouth. He looked apologetically to Hickok and smiled. "I'm sounding like a preacher again, aren't I? Excuse me."

Hickok waved his hand. "No excuses necessary, Reverend," he said. "You're right. I reckon most of these fellows taking wagers on war haven't ever been in one themselves. Short or long, war is a terrible thing. Even when the cause is just, like it is now."

"You won't get killed?" Luke asked Hickok anxiously.

Hickok answered bluntly. "Ain't no way to know, one way or the other."

"I want to join up with Lincoln, too," Luke said with sudden resolve. "I want to shoot me some rebels."

Hickok cuffed Luke playfully on the back of the neck. "You got plenty of work ahead of you just to grow up, Luke."

"Mr. Hickok's right," Parson Harte said. "Besides, war is no place for a boy."

"Won't you miss the pony express?" Luke persisted. "And what about Bill Cody? Do you think he'll join up with the Union army, too?" Hickok smiled.

"Well, Luke," Hickok mused, "as to the plans of Mr. William F. Cody, I really couldn't say. But the plain truth of the matter is the pony express rider is an idea whose time has come and gone. The country's changed. Telegraph wires are going up all over this territory. They're faster and cheaper. Ain't no use for us anymore." Hickok spoke plainly and without any hint of regret or remorse.

The rest of the evening passed pleasantly in agreeable conversation, though the knowledge that it was their last together brought a kind of gloom that hung on each of them like a heavy weight.

It was Hickok who finally brought the evening to an end. Both Luke and Parson Harte understood that Hickok was not a man comfortable with easy familiarities. So as not to embarrass him, they did not elaborate on his departure with tears or hugs. Hickok gathered his hat and his fiddle and with a familiar tilt of his head mumbled his thanks and farewell.

From the porch Luke watched Hickok hoist himself into the saddle. Hickok slipped on his hat and pulled it down tight. Despite his promise to himself, Luke felt tears welling up in his eyes.

Hickok pulled something from his saddlebag and motioned for Luke. The boy jumped down from the porch and reached for the packet. "Something for you to remember me by," Hickok said.

Luke unfolded the leather packet and stared at the gleaming bowie knife.

"It's your knife," Luke said in disbelief. "The one you killed the grizzly bear with."

Hickok laughed and gave the boy's head a shake. "Like I done tried to tell both you and Mr. Cody—it weren't a grizzly bear, it was a *cinnamon!*"

Luke hiccuped a laugh and wiped awkwardly at his eyes with his shirtsleeve. Luke promised Hickok that he'd remember.

Hickok gave Luke a short wave and a neat tip of the hat, snapped the reins once, and instantly Nell turned and broke into a gallop.

"Good luck!" Parson Harte called after him. He waved. Already Hickok was a dim silhouette on the horizon. Then he was gone.

Parson Harte put his arm around Luke's shoulders and gave him a squeeze.

"He sure is something, isn't he?"

Luke managed a smile. "He sure is."

EPILOG

James Butler Hickok was born in 1837 in Homer (now known as Troy Grove), Illinois. In 1856 he went to Kansas. There he joined the antislavery Free State Army and later became constable in Monticello Township. He worked as a stagecoach driver for a short time on the Sante Fe and Oregon trails, and in 1861 he was sent to the pony express station at Rock Creek, Nebraska, reportedly to recover from an attack by a bear.

Hickok tangled with some bullies that summer and, in what he claimed was self-defense, shot three of them, killing one. Jack Chambers and his gang, however, are fictional.

Recognizing that the introduction of the telegraph in 1861 would make the pony express obsolete, Hickok became wagon master of a Union army supply train in the Civil War. At this time, Hickok apparently acquired the nickname Wild Bill defending a bartender against a group of rowdy drunks in Independence, Missouri. For the remainder of the war, Hickok was a spy and a scout. He returned to Kansas after the war and fought against the Indians and scouted for Lieutenant Colonel George Armstrong Custer.

In 1871, Hickok became marshal of Abilene, Kansas, a cow town notorious for its lawless rampages by rowdy, gun-wielding cowboys. Hickok helped tame Abilene by enforcing a ban on guns from city streets. In a fatal gunfight one evening with a gambler who refused to surrender his weapon, Hickok accidentally shot and killed a special policeman. It was an incident that reportedly weighed so heavily on Hickok that he never killed a man again.

Hickok tried running his own Wild West show but never was as successful as his good friend William F. Cody. In 1876, Hickok followed the gold rush to Deadwood in the Black Hills of the Dakota Territory. There he met Calamity Jane.

It was also in Deadwood that a man named Jack McCall walked up behind Hickok, then thirty-nine years old, and shot him in the head during a poker game. McCall claimed the murder was an act of revenge on behalf of his brother. However, others insisted McCall was hired as an assassin by John Barnes, a man with whom Hickok had had an earlier disagreement.

Among the cards that spilled from Hickok's hands as he was shot were a pair of aces and a pair of eights—what would become known as the Deadman's Hand.